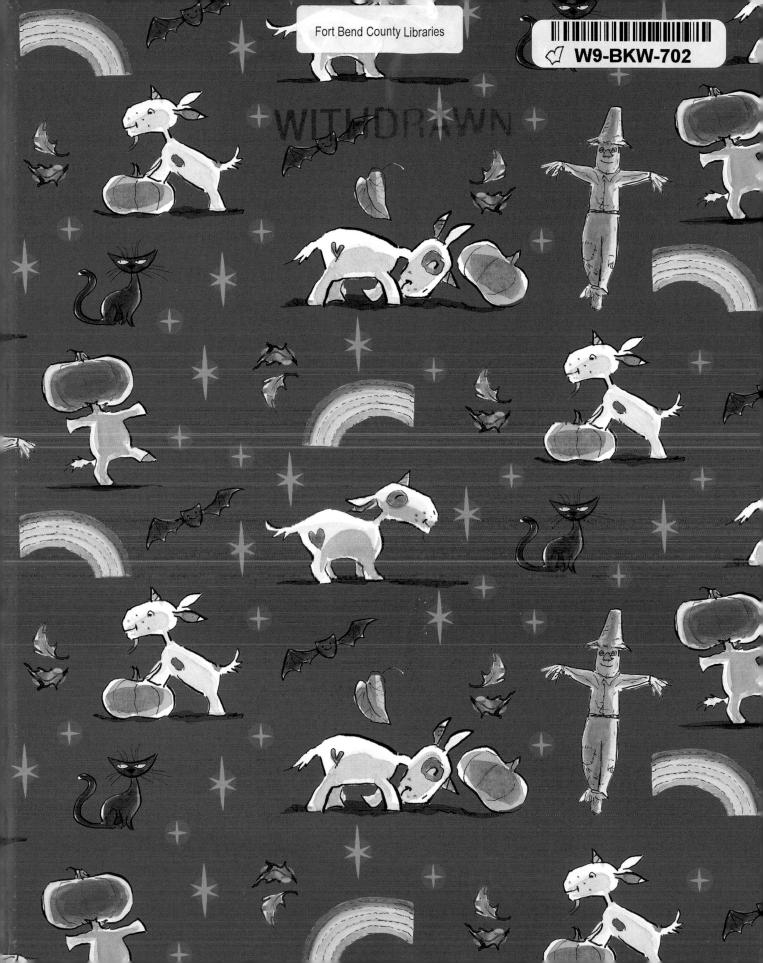

To the students at Edgewood School in Muskegon Heights

Farrar Straus Giroux Books for Young Readers
An imprint of Macmillan Publishing Group, LLC
120 Broadway, New York, NY 10271

Copyright © 2020 by Amy Young
All rights reserved
Color separations by Bright Arts (H.K.) Ltd.
Printed in China by Toppan Leefung Printing Ltd.,
Dongguan City, Guangdong Province
Designed by Monique Sterling
First edition, 2020

1 3 5 7 9 10 8 6 4 2

mackids.com

Library of Congress Control Number: 2019948846
ISBN: 978-0-374-30850-6

Our books may be purchased in bulk for promotional, educational, or business use. Please contact
your local bookseller or the Macmillan Corporate and Premium Sales Department at
(800) 221-7945 ext. 5442 or by email at MacmillanSpecialMarkets@macmillan.com.

A Unicorn Named SPARKLE and the Pumpkin Monster

Amy Young

FARRAR STRAUS GIROUX
NEW YORK

Lucy and her pet unicorn, Sparkle, were going to Pat's Pumpkin Farm. The air was crisp and Sparkle felt frisky.

They went into the corn maze. Sparkle got lost and
tried to eat his way out. Lucy had to rescue him.

They played games. Sparkle's favorite game was
Grab-the-Donut. He grabbed a lot of them.

There was cider and cupcakes. Sparkle loved cupcakes.
He loved them so much that he ate ten of them, and then
he drank a whole bucket of cider.

Next it was time to go pick a pumpkin.

"Sparkle, look at that tree. It's kind of spooky, isn't it?"

Sparkle thought it was very spooky.

"And look at that creepy scarecrow!" said Lucy. "Sometimes it's fun to feel scared, right?"

Sparkle wasn't so sure.

Lucy chose a smooth, round pumpkin. Sparkle chose a pumpkin that was as big as his head.

B·E·E·E·H!

Oh, Sparkle, you're so silly!

He had trouble carrying it.

When they got back to the barn, it was time to decorate.
Sparkle made his pumpkin cheerful and happy.

Lucy made her pumpkin scary. "Sparkle, look!"

Sparkle was terrified.

BACK!

Lucy said, "**WAIT, Sparkle, it's just me!**"
But Sparkle had already bolted out of the barn.

Sparkle hid behind a pile of pumpkins. He stayed very still and tried to make himself small.

At first it was quiet. But then he heard:

AAAAAAAAAAAAAAA

It's a pumpkin monster, he thought. What should I do?

He saw a big pumpkin beside him, and he had
an idea. He carved a little door with his horn.

He scooped out the seeds and
jumped inside as fast as he could.

Sparkle heard the noise again. It was not as loud from inside the pumpkin, but he could tell it was coming closer and closer.

The monster was going to get him!

Sparkle was so afraid that he tried to run, even though he was still inside the pumpkin. The pumpkin rocked and lurched, and then it broke off the vine.

It started to roll and bump through the field, with Sparkle inside.

When it got to a little hill, the pumpkin rolled faster.

Sparkle couldn't stop it.

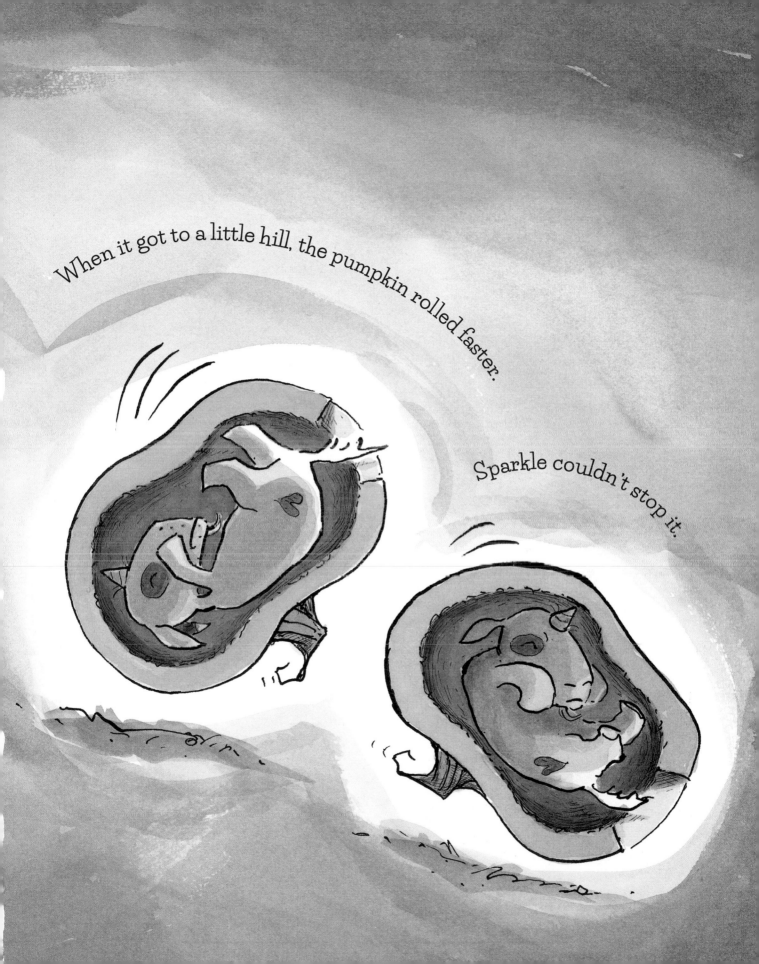

Meanwhile, Lucy had been looking for Sparkle this whole time.

Suddenly she saw a great big pumpkin rolling
and bouncing and bumping toward her.

"Help!" she yelped. "It's a pumpkin monster!"

It was just about to flatten her like a pancake, but at the last second it landed on a sharp rock.

It burst open, and there was Sparkle.
"B-E-E-E-E-H!"

Lucy laughed and said, "Ha! I scared you and you scared me! Isn't that hilarious?"

"Oh no, you're still afraid, aren't you? I'm sorry! Today was supposed to be fun."

"I hope you can forgive me for scaring you."

Lucy gave Sparkle a kiss on the nose.
He forgave her right away.

Then she said, "It's dark. How are we going
to see to get back to the barn?"

A huge, happy rainbow blazed out of
Sparkle's horn. It lit up the whole field.
It was easy to find their way back.

They were just in time for the bonfire. Sparkle used his horn to cook two perfect marshmallows in the crackling flames, one for himself, and one for Lucy.

Lucy said, "You are such a good friend to me. I won't ever try to scare you again, because I want to be a good friend to you."

Sparkle sighed happily. He ate one more marshmallow and three more donuts. Then he fell fast asleep, with his head in Lucy's lap.

"Sweet dreams, Sparkle."

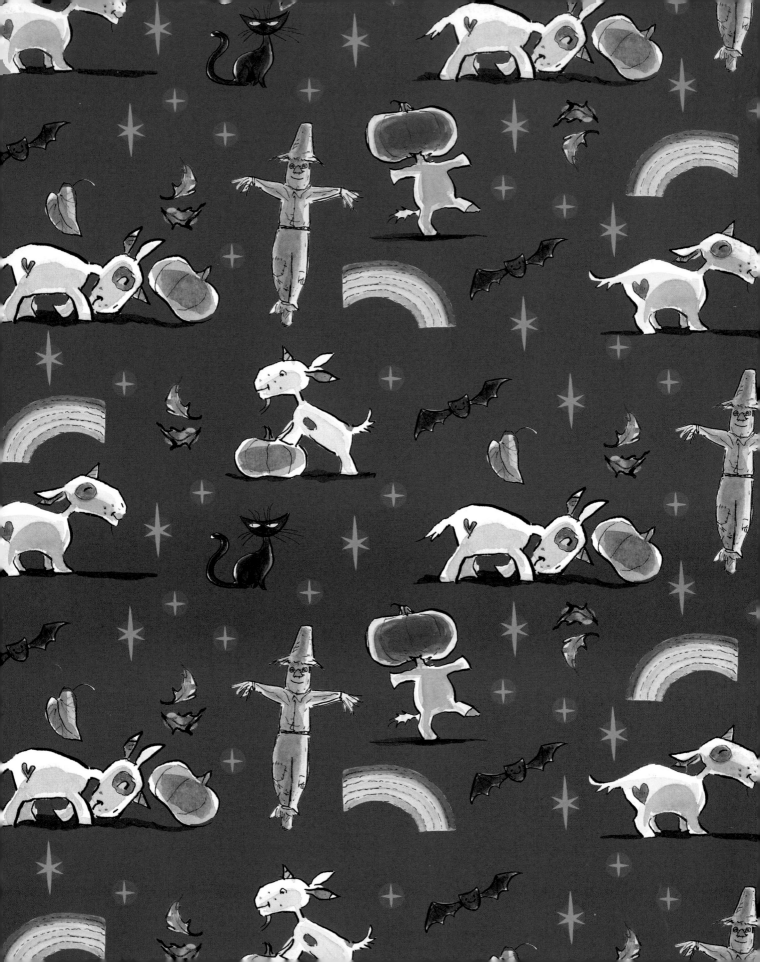